T

The Three Witches

Collected by

Zora Neale Hurston

Adapted by

Joyce Carol Thomas

Illustrated by

Faith Ringgold

HarperCollins*Publishers*

THREE WITCHES HAD ALREADY EATEN a boy and girl's mother and father, so their grandmother took them to live with her far off in the woods.

Grandma loved the children and they loved her. They had many happy times together.

One morning Grandma said, "Our cupboard's getting low. I'll go fetch us some more food." She wrapped a shawl around her hunched shoulders. "I should be back by dusk."

Grandma was gone a long, long time, and the boy and girl became very hungry.

So the boy said, "I'll go to the cellar and see if there's anything left for us to eat."

When the boy came up from the cellar and saw his sister walking all over the house, he asked, "What's the matter?"

"I smell witches," she said.

"Good ones or bad ones?"

"Bad," she whispered.

Her brother looked around, but he didn't see any witches. He showed her the last of the yams he had found.

"I'll bake them." She shoved them in the oven.

When they were done, the boy buttered them.

"Delicious," they said as they began eating the warm yams.

While they were eating the last yam, sure enough in came three witches.

"Let's eat these children," said the three witches.

"Oh, please don't!" the children cried. "Wait 'til Grandma comes. She'll feed you!"

"When will your grandma be back?" asked the witches.

"By sundown," said the boy.

"No, we can't wait," said the first witch.

"We won't eat you if you go get some water from the spring to fill our bellies," said the second witch.

"All right," said the shaking children.

So the third witch gave them a sieve to fill with water.

"If you don't return at once," all three said, "we'll eat you up immediately!"

The boy and girl went to the spring for the water. They dipped and dipped to try to fill the sieve, but the water always ran out of the holes faster than they could fill it.

At last they saw the three witches coming to the spring. Those witches! Their teeth were far longer than their lips!

The boy and the girl were *sooo* scared.

The boy grabbed his sister's hand and said, "Let's run! Let's go 'cross the deep river! They can't follow us there!"

The children ran as fast as they could.

They saw the three witches behind them coming so fast that they made a great cloud of dust that darkened the sun.

The boy stumbled. He and his sister realized they could not reach the river before the witches got to them. So they climbed a big, tall tree.

Hail Counter!
Hail Jack!
Hail Hickory!
Block eye chip
block eye chip
Whyncher
O-ooo! Whyncher

The witches followed the smell of the children's blood until they stopped at the foot of the tree. They looked up and spied the boy and girl.

The three witches picked up three broad-axes and began to chop down the tree.

"O-ooo! Whyncher, whyncher!

"O-ooo! Whyncher, whyncher!"

The girl said:

"Block eye, chip! Block eye, chip!"

And the pieces that the witches chopped off flew back into their eyes and blinded them.

The boy called his three hounds, Counter, Jack, and Hickory:

"Hail, Counter! Hail, Jack! Hail, Hickory!

"Hail, Counter! Hail, Jack! Hail, Hickory!"

Now the three blind witches were at the tree trunk, swinging their three broadaxes and chopping away.

"O-ooo! Whyncher, whyncher!

"O-ooo! Whyncher, whyncher!"

And so it went back and forth like that, the boy calling the dogs and the blind witches chopping and the girl chanting.

"Hail, Counter! Hail, Jack! Hail, Hickory!"

"O-ooo! Whyncher, whyncher!"

"Block eye, chip! Block eye, chip!"

The tree was beginning to tip over, and the children were *sooo, sooo* scared.

But the boy kept on calling:

"Hail, Counter! Hail, Jack! Hail, Hickory!"

The girl kept on chanting:

"Block eye, chip! Block eye, chip!"

The witches, getting blinder and blinder, kept it up:

"O-ooo! Whyncher, whyncher!"

Block eye chip
Hail Counter! Hail Jack!
Hail Hickory!
Block eye chip
o-ooo!
Whyncher whyncher

The girl asked her brother, "Do you see the hounds coming yet?"

He said, "Not yet." He hollered:

"Hail, Counter! Hail, Jack! Hail, Hickory!"

He didn't see the dogs coming, so he began to sing:

"We're lost out here all by ourselves."

The girl chanted:

"Block eye, chip! Block eye, chip."

Hailcounter!
HAIL Jack
Hail Hickory
Blackeyechip
Blackeyechip!
O-ooo!
Whyncher
Whyncher

Back at Grandma's house, the hound dogs, Counter, Jack, and Hickory, were tied up in the yard.

Grandma hauled a bag of food up the steps. She was exhausted from her journey. She wondered where the children were, but she was so tired that she fell fast asleep.

The three hounds could hear the children. They wanted to run and help, but they couldn't get loose.

And Grandma, who was snoring, couldn't hear the dogs whining.

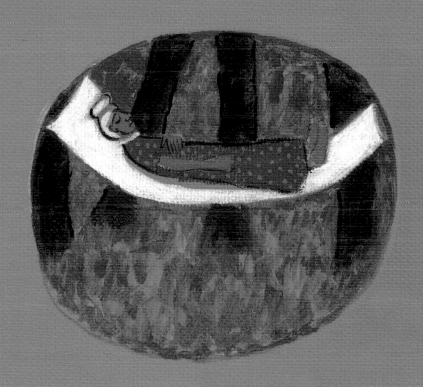

But a black-and-white snake heard the children and ran to the house. He crawled up to Grandma and slapped her across the face with his tail.

Grandma woke up and loosed the dogs.

"We're lost out here all by ourselves."
"O-ooo! Whyncher, whyncher!"
"Block eye, chip! Block eye, chip!"
By that time here came the dogs.

The tree was leaning over toppling, with the
children almost in reach of the three witches.
  The girl and boy were *sooo* glad to see the dogs.
  The boy told Counter, "Kill the witches!"
  The girl told Jack, "Suck their blood!"
  They both told Hickory, "Eat the bones!"

By that time I left.

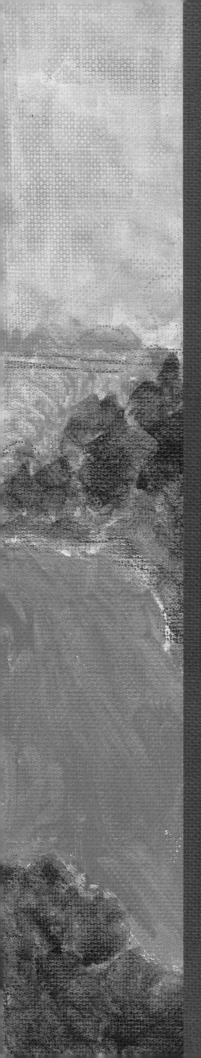

Adapter's Note

Now we're out on a limb gasping at three blind witches hacking away at the tree trunk.

Teeth longer than their lips! Now that's scary and funny at the same time.

Our hearts thump even as we snuggle with a book, laughing in our beds or at our desks, hunted by three witches.

Who knew better than Zora Neale Hurston about the tickling terrors lurking in scary places?

And those hound dogs begging to save us, struggling against the ropes, until Grandma, awakened by a snake's slap, leaps up out of her bed and sets the dogs free.

Well, children, believe I'll bake three extra yams just in case the witches stop by here, so I can feed them.

—Joyce Carol Thomas

Illustrator's Note

I absolutely loved illustrating this book. Zora Neale Hurston is my favorite storyteller in the whole world. If someone had asked me whose stories (other than my own) I would most enjoy illustrating, I would have shouted Zora Neale Hurston, for she can spin a tale better than anyone else I know. Thanks, Phoebe, for making a precious dream come true.

We can never thank Zora enough for her brilliant research and collection of the great African American oral tradition. To be sure, a lot of these stories would have been lost without her vision. She has such wit, sheer genius and charm. Like Maya Angelou, our present-day storytelling guru, Zora will keep us reading and laughing for centuries to come.

Whenever I have a need to laugh and have nothing fun to engage me, I pop Zora's tape *Of Mules and Men* into my tape deck, and wherever I am, I am laughing just like I never heard it before.

—Faith Ringgold

Zora Neale Hurston
1891—1960

To my nephew, Michael Mwandishi Haynes
—J.C.T.

This book is dedicated to the endearing imagination of childhood and the evil ole witches who playfully scared us all when we were kids. Childhood, the most wonderful time of life, is so much fun and much too short to waste. So take your book and a flashlight and head under the covers so the wicked ole witches can't find you. Enjoy!

—F.R.

The Zora Neale Hurston Trust gratefully thanks Faith Ringgold for her superb work. The Trust is also very thankful for the vision and guidance of Susan Katz, Kate Jackson, and our wonderful editor, Phoebe Yeh. Lastly, our continued appreciation of Cathy Hemming, who initially brought us to HarperCollins Children's Books, and Jane Friedman and everyone at HarperCollins who works tirelessly on behalf of Zora.

Source as it appeared in *Every Tongue Got to Confess: Negro Folk-Tales from the Gulf States*: Hattie Reeves, born on Island of Grand Command, West Indies; about 50; domestic.

On page 29, Zora Neale Hurston delights us by using a Caribbean-flavored expression: "By that time I left" means "The End."
—J.C.T.